Caring for Your Magical Pets

Taking Care of Your Phoenix

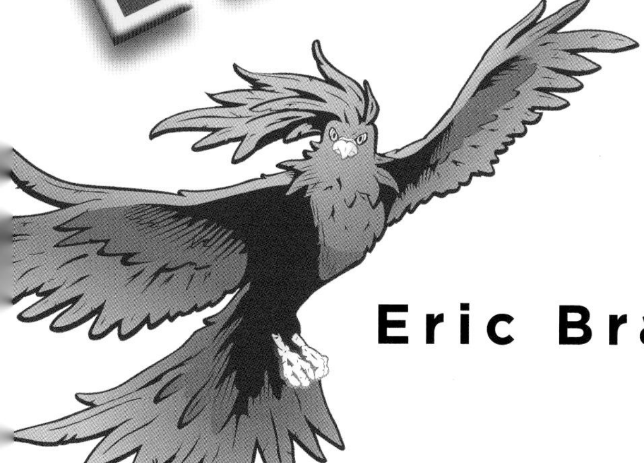

Eric Braun

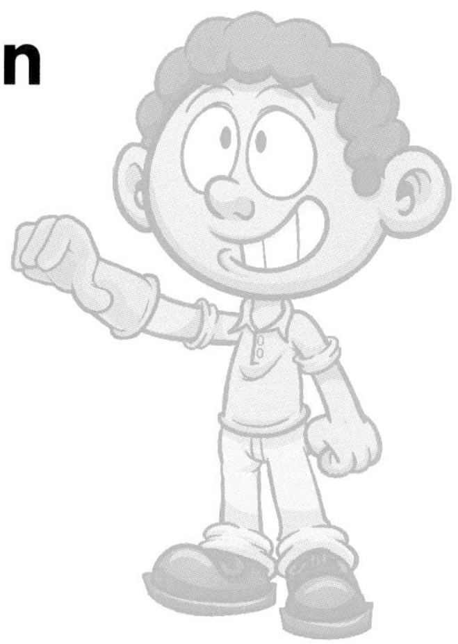

BLACK RABBIT BOOKS

Hi Jinx is published by Black Rabbit Books
P.O. Box 3263, Mankato, Minnesota, 56002.
www.blackrabbitbooks.com
Copyright © 2020 Black Rabbit Books

Marysa Storm, editor; Michael Sellner, designer;
Omay Ayres, photo researcher

Library of Congress Cataloging-in-Publication Data
Names: Braun, Eric, 1971- author, illustrator.
Title: Taking care of your phoenix / by Eric Braun.
Description: Mankato, Minnesota : Black Rabbit Books, [2020] | Series:
Hi Jinx. Caring for your magical pets | Summary: Provides easy-to-read
instructions for choosing and caring for a pet phoenix, such as the
importance of playing with it several times a day. Includes discussion
questions. | Includes bibliographical references and index.
Identifiers: LCCN 2018043631 (print) | LCCN 2018052543 (ebook) |
ISBN 9781680729184 (e-book) | ISBN 9781680729122 (library binding) |
ISBN 9781644660911 (paperback)
Subjects: | CYAC: Phoenix (Mythical bird)–Fiction. | Pets–Fiction.
Classification: LCC PZ7.1.B751542 (ebook) | LCC PZ7.1.B751542
Tap 2020 (print) | DDC [E]–dc23
LC record available at https://lccn.loc.gov/2018043631

Printed in the United States. 9/19

Image Credits

Dreamstime: Danilo Sanino, Cover (phoenix), 12 (phoenix); Shutterstock: Alena
Kozlova, 16–17 (hill); AlexeyZet, 16–17 (house); Aluna1, 19 (bkgd); Amanda
Tromley, 1 (phoenix), 18–19 (phoenix); Angeliki Vel, 18 (sun), 20 (grass); ekler,
10; Ellerslie, 6–7; Freestyle_stock_photo, Cover (bkgd), 12 (bkgd); frescomovie,
Back Cover (bkgd), 3 (bkgd), 15 (bkgd), 21 (bkgd); GB_Art, 1 (glove), 19 (glove);
GraphicCrazy, 11 (phoenix), 16 (phoenix); GraphicsRF, 15 (top bkgd, top boy, btm
kids, bkgd); larryrains, 11 (nest); lawang design, 2–3; Lilu330, Cover (feathers),
12 (feathers); Lorelyn Medina, 5 (kids); mejnak, 4–5; Memo Angeles, Cover
(kids), 1 (boy), 8, 12 (kids), 19 (boy), 20 (bird); Oguz Aral, Cover
(treehouse), 12 (treehouse); opicobello, 13 (tear), 14, 19 (marker strokes);
Padma Sanjaya, 20 (flaming stick); Pasko Maksim, Back Cover (tear), 23
(tear), 24; pitju, 17 (page curl), 21 (page curl); Ron Dale, 5 (marker
stroke), 6 (marker stroke), 13 (marker stroke), 20 (marker stroke);
Sararoom Design, 16 (left mouse), 17 (mouse), 21 (mouse);
satori.artwork, 4 (phoenix); Shamzami, 15 (top phoenix);
Studio_G, 12 (tree); sundatoon, 16 (large mouse);
Tueris, 5 (marker stroke); umnola, 15 (btm phoenix);
vectorpouch, 15 (ball); your, 17 (clouds) Every
effort has been made to contact copyright
holders for material reproduced
in this book. Any omissions
will be rectified in
subsequent printings
if notice is given to
the publisher.

contents

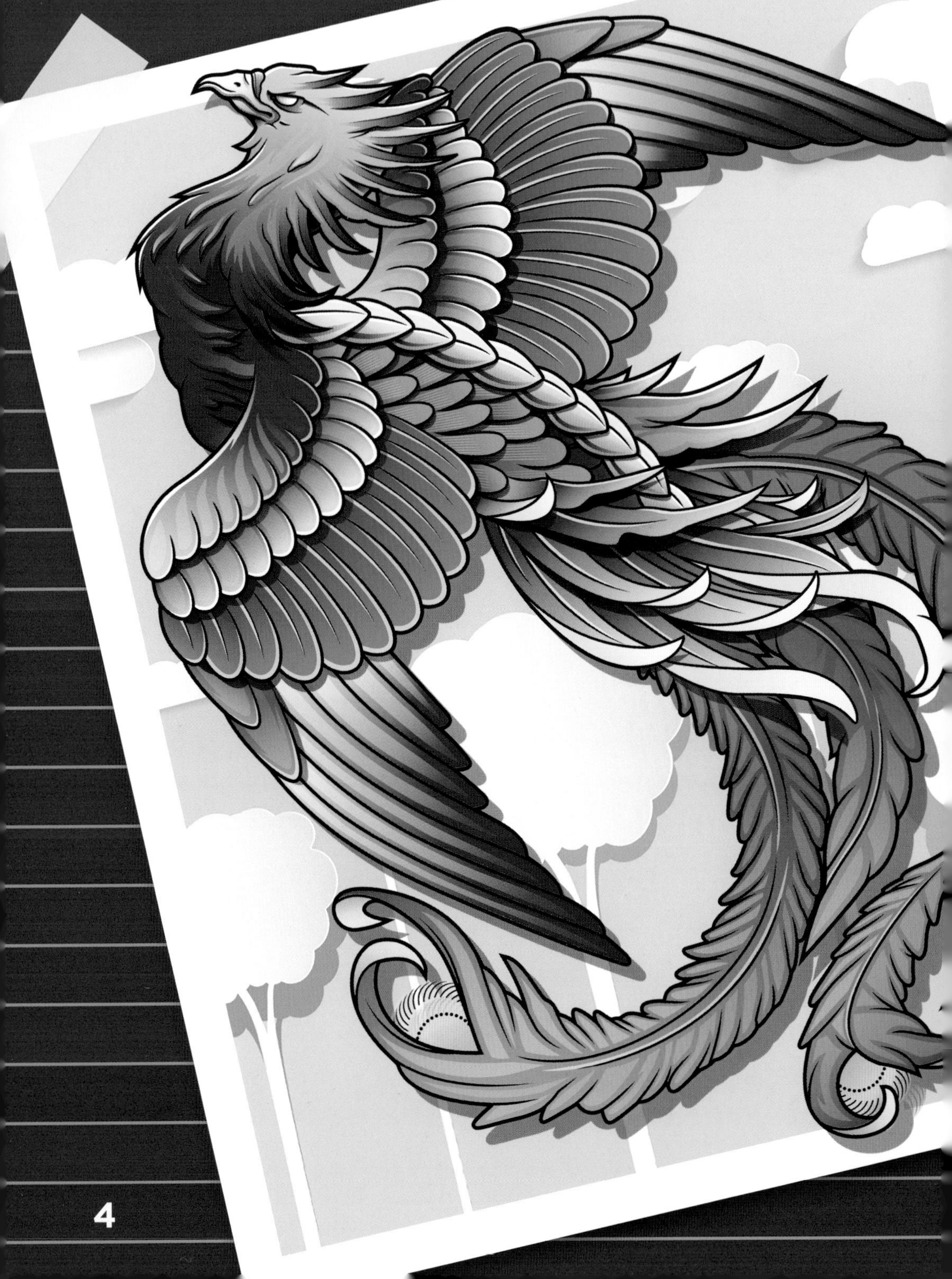

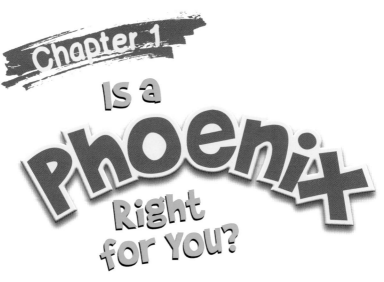

Chapter 1

Is a Phoenix Right for You?

A phoenix flies through the sky, showing off its colorful feathers. A bright light **radiates** from them. People gasp at the bird's beauty. They wonder who could be lucky enough to have such a pet.

Phoenixes are magical birds. They're also incredible pets. But taking care of a phoenix isn't easy. You should know what you're getting into before bringing one home.

5

Chapter 2
Understanding Your Phoenix

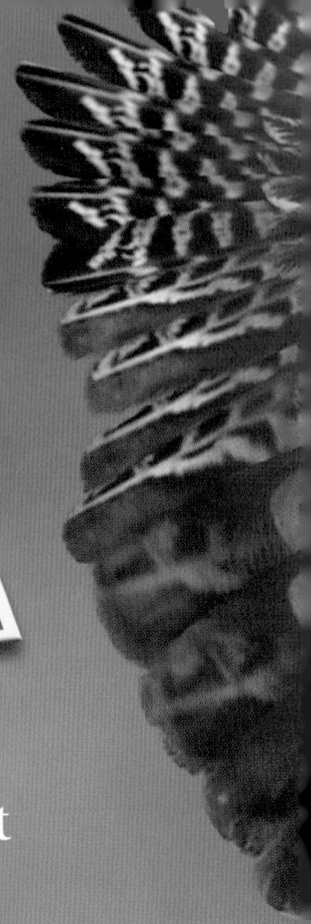

Before getting a phoenix, you must understand it. Most have gold or red feathers. All have eyes that shine like the sun. A phoenix is beautiful. And it *knows* it.

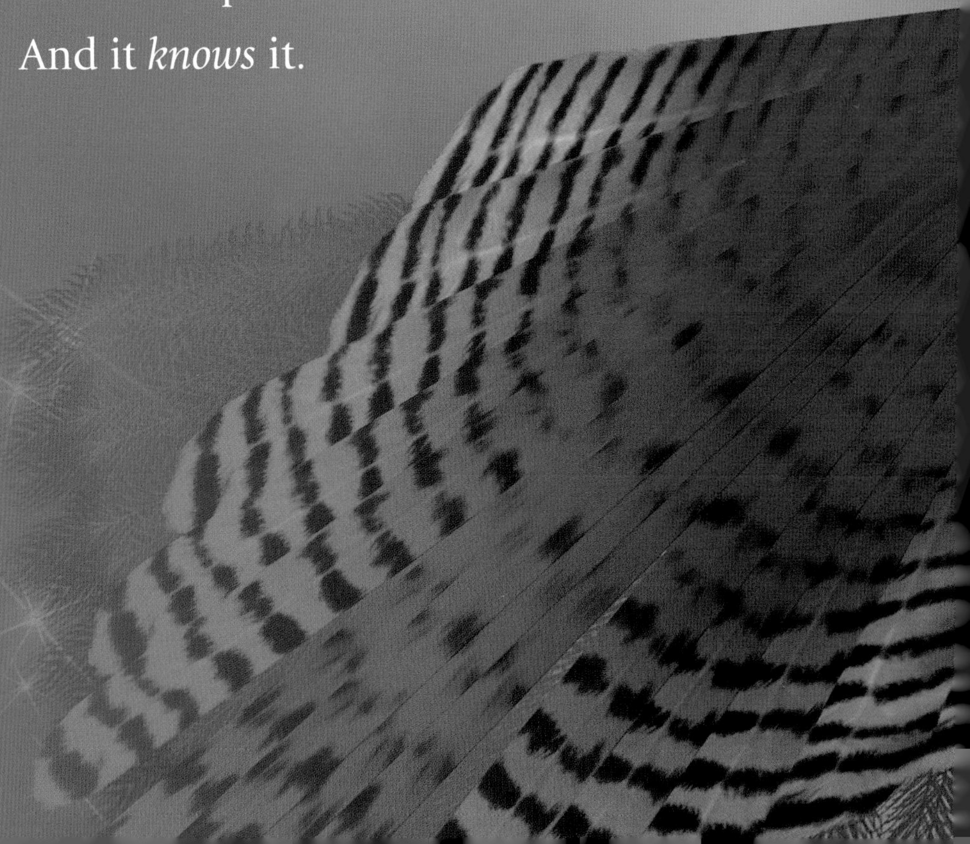

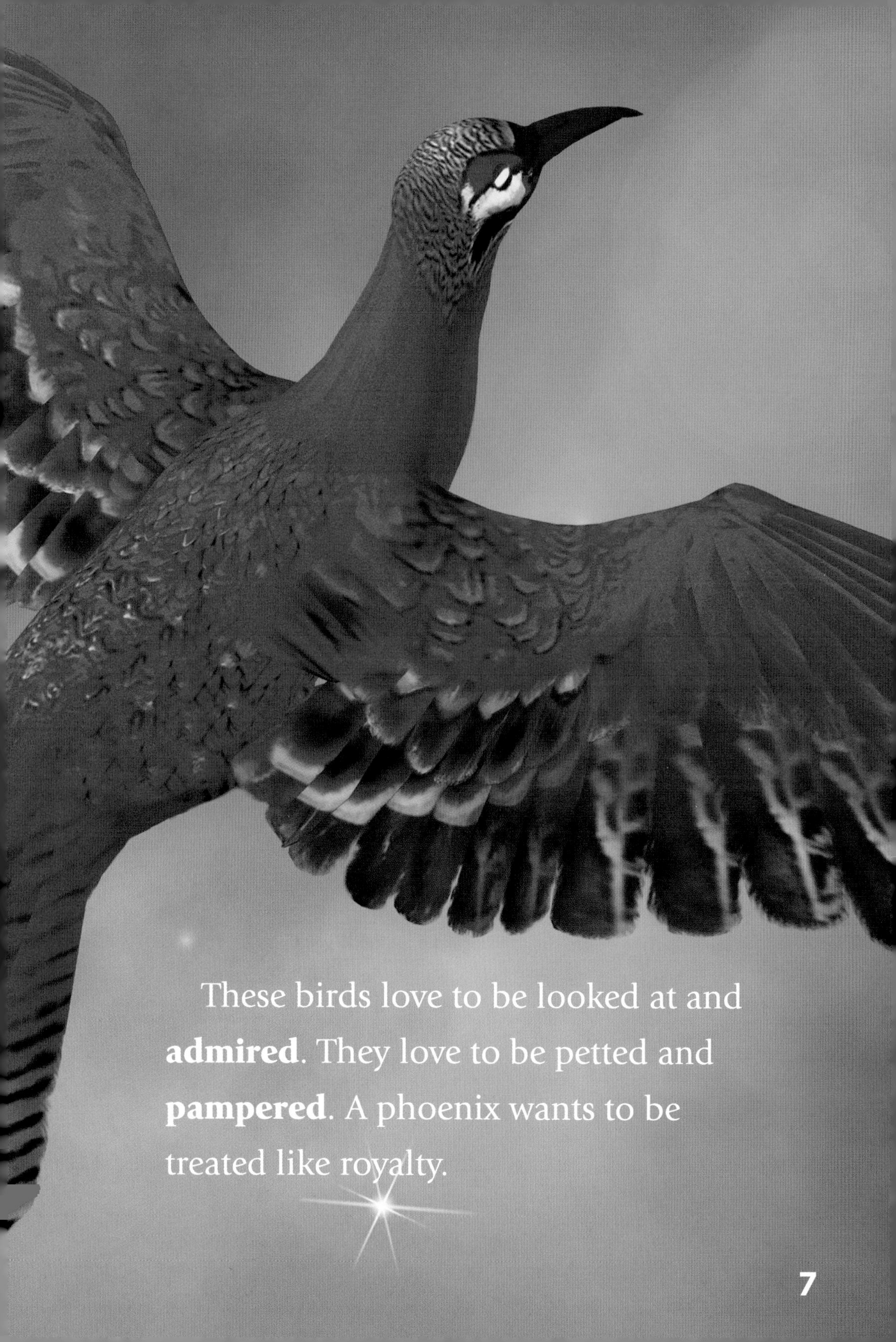

These birds love to be looked at and **admired**. They love to be petted and **pampered**. A phoenix wants to be treated like royalty.

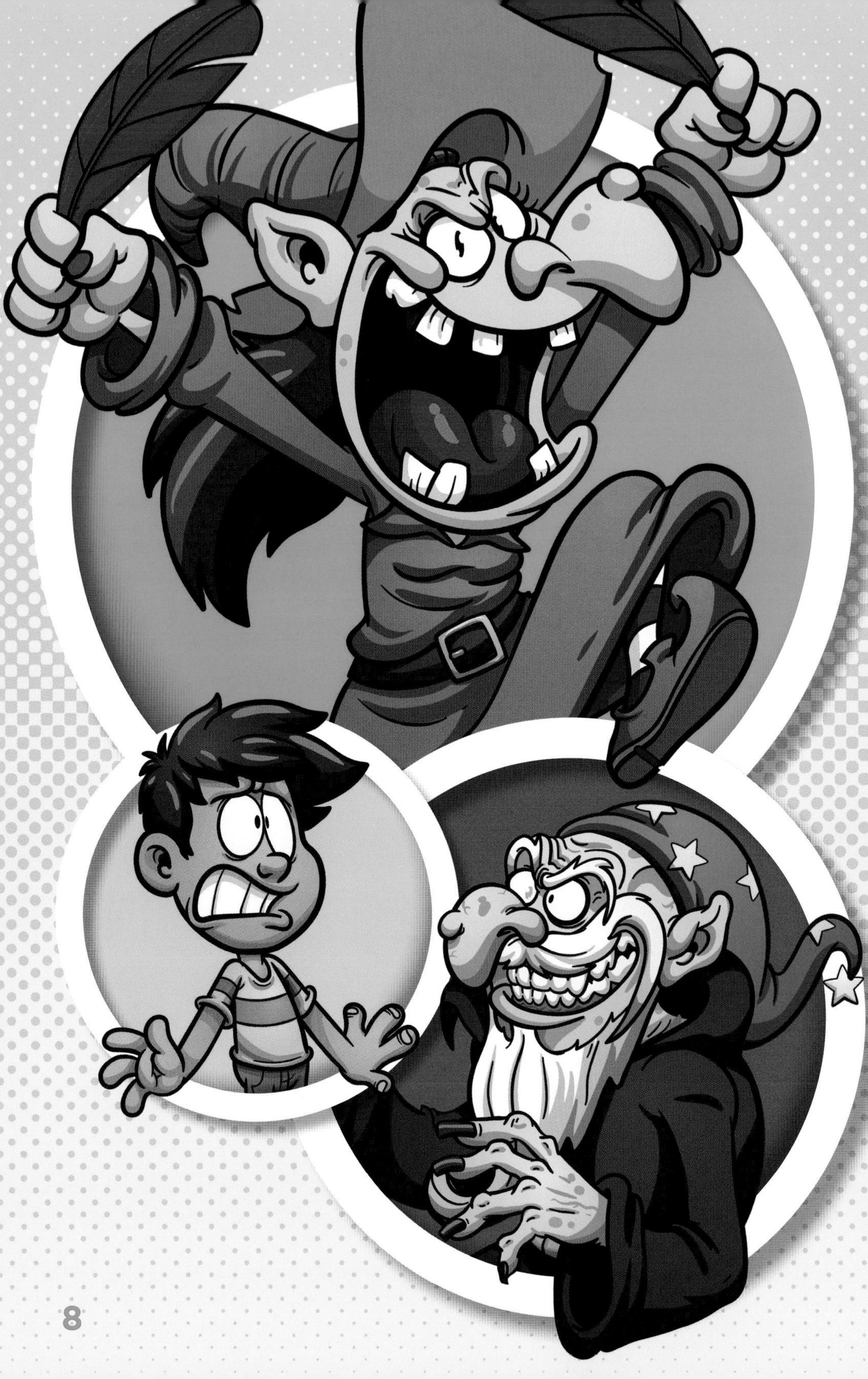

Magic and Meaning

Phoenixes are **mystical**. That makes them popular with magic folks. Wizards and witches often want their feathers for spells. They might want to read the birds' droppings. They're looking for messages in the poop. If you have a phoenix, you might get visits from these people.

You'll want to make a plan for visitors. Have strict visiting hours. Try charging an entry fee to make some extra money.

Long Life and New Life

A phoenix can live more than 1,000 years. When it's ready to die, it builds a nest. The phoenix then bursts into flame and burns up. Out of the ashes, the phoenix is reborn. This process happens about every 100 years.

It's easy to tell if your phoenix is getting ready to burn up. The bird's color will fade. Its feathers will start to fall out too. Don't worry when this happens.

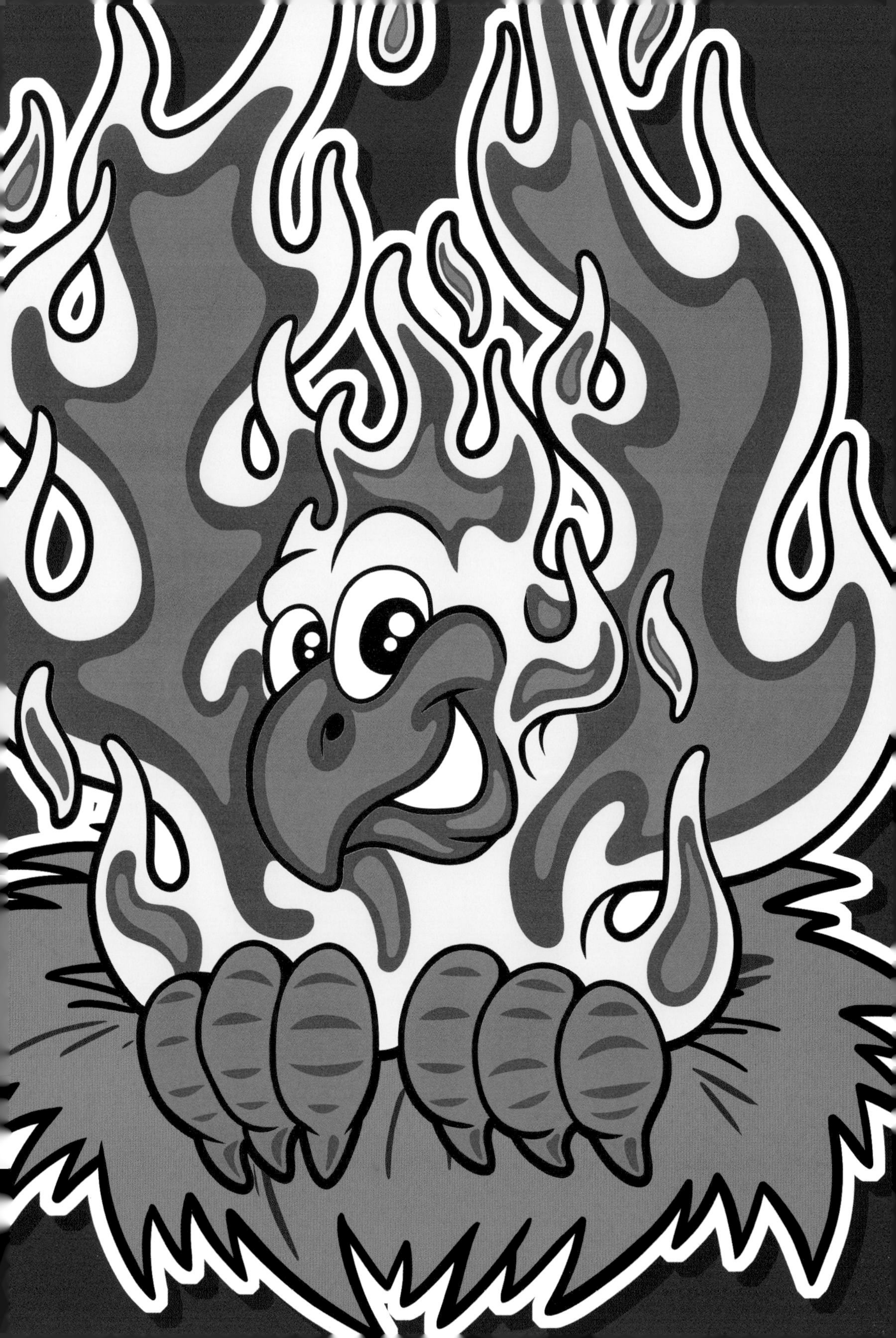

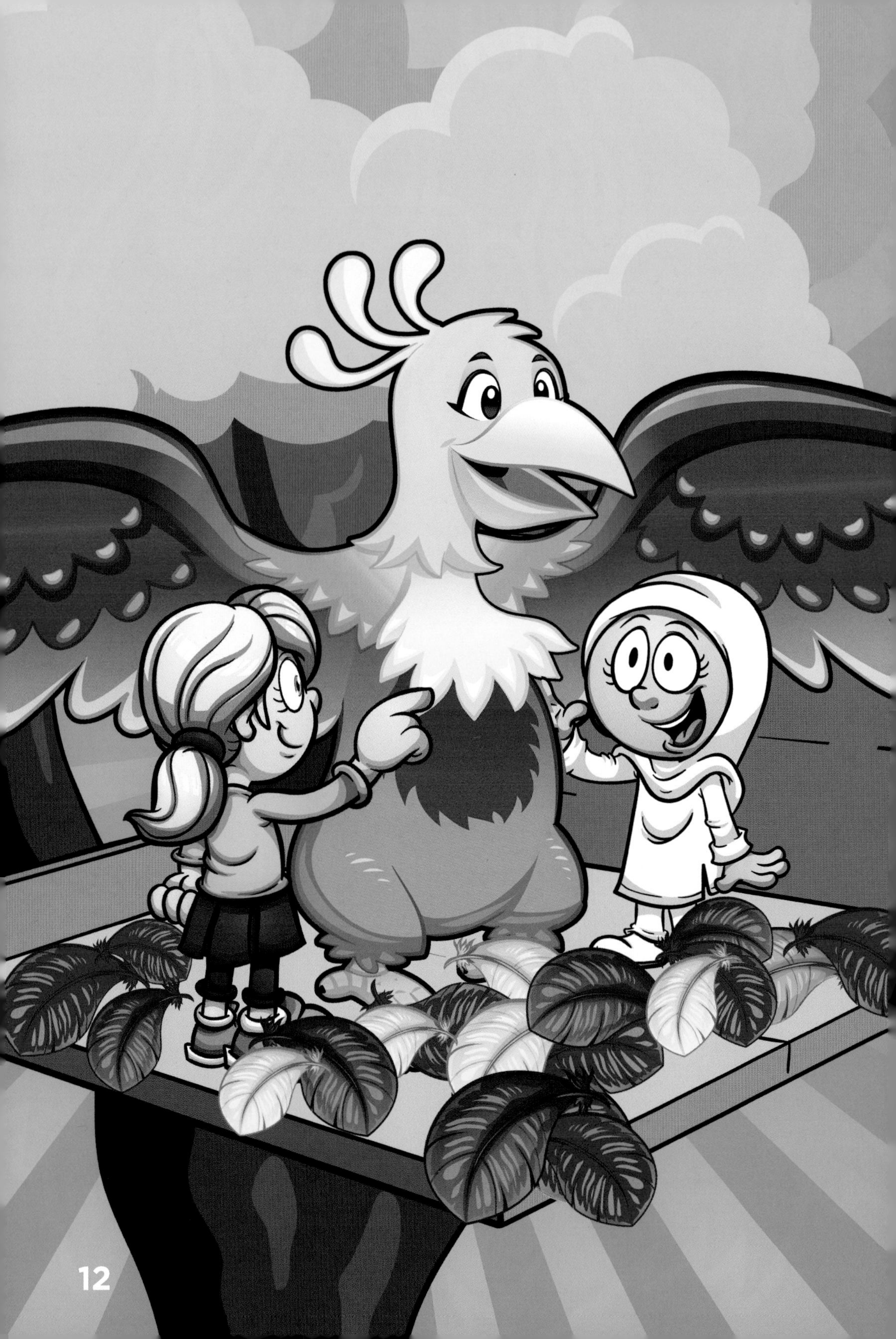

Chapter 3
Caring for Your Phoenix

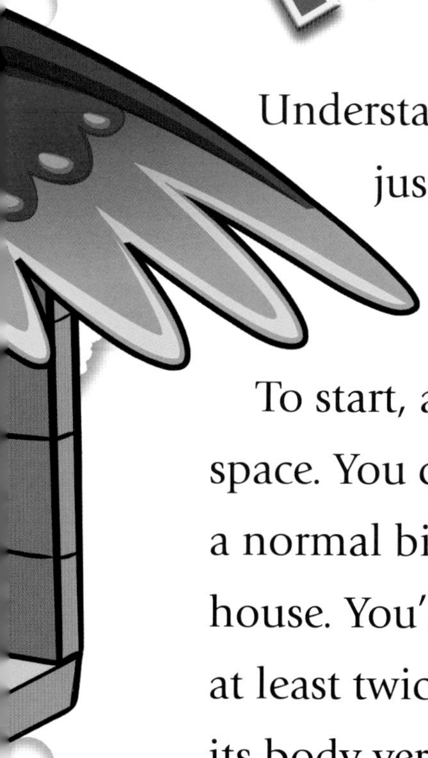

Understanding your phoenix is just the beginning. You also need to know how to care for it!

To start, a phoenix needs its own space. You can't keep it in a cage like a normal bird. Instead, give it a tree house. You'll need to clean the house at least twice a week. A phoenix keeps its body very clean. But it makes a mess of its environment. Regular cleaning keeps layers of poop and feathers from building up.

Exercise and Play

A phoenix needs lots of activity to stay happy and healthy. Play with it often. Five or six times a day is good. Play for 10 minutes or more each time. These birds enjoy games like fetch. Phoenixes also like playing games of hide-and-seek. Their colorful feathers do make them easy to find, though. You should pretend it's hard, and take your time. It'll be fun for your pet.

If your phoenix doesn't get enough attention, it'll squawk and squawk.

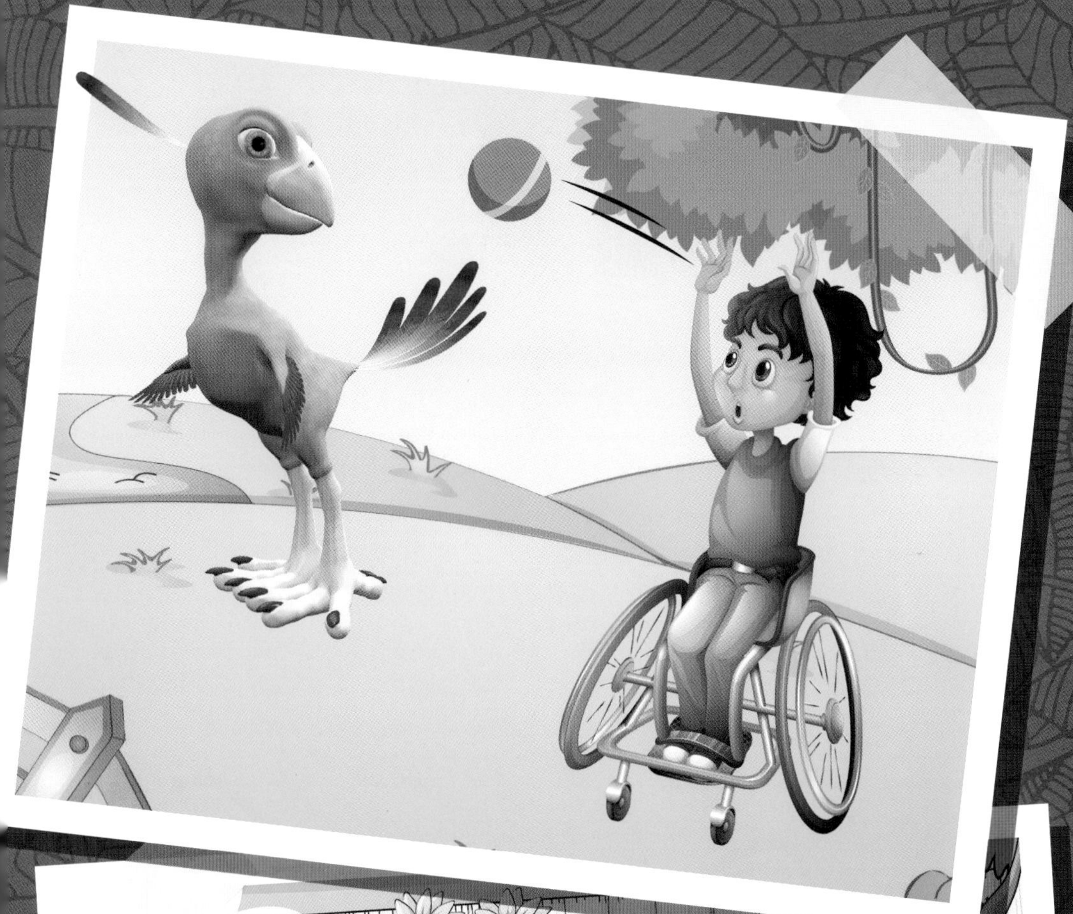

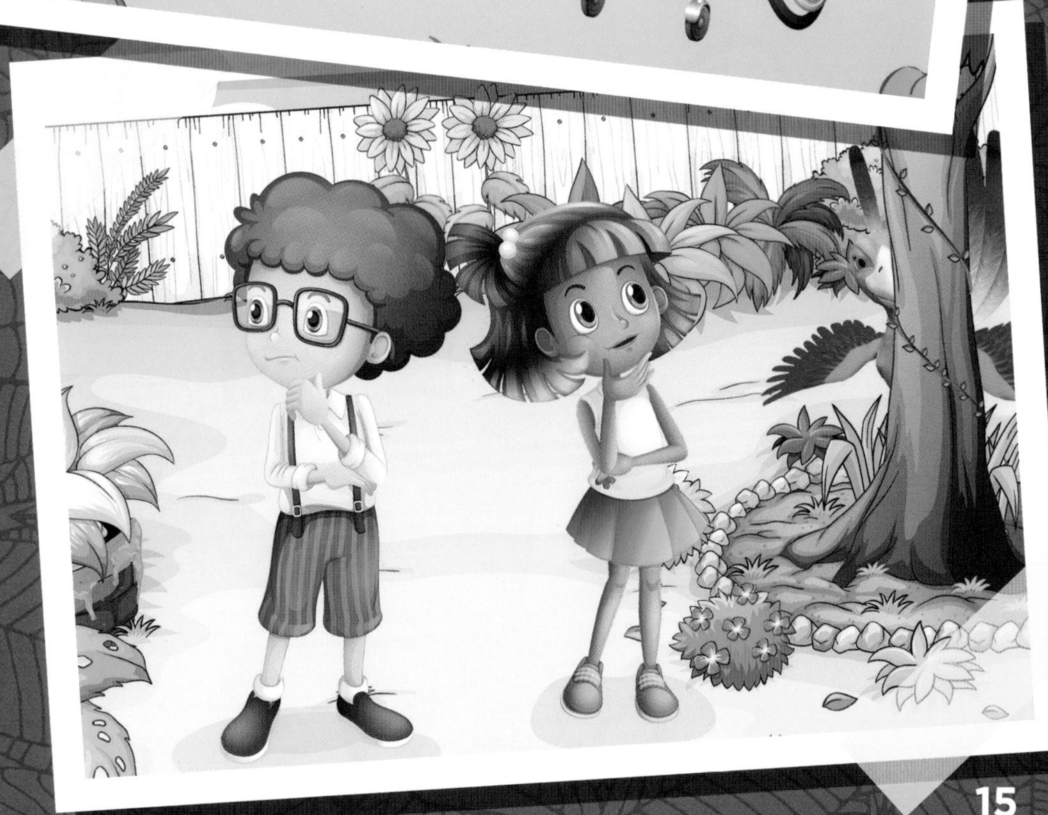

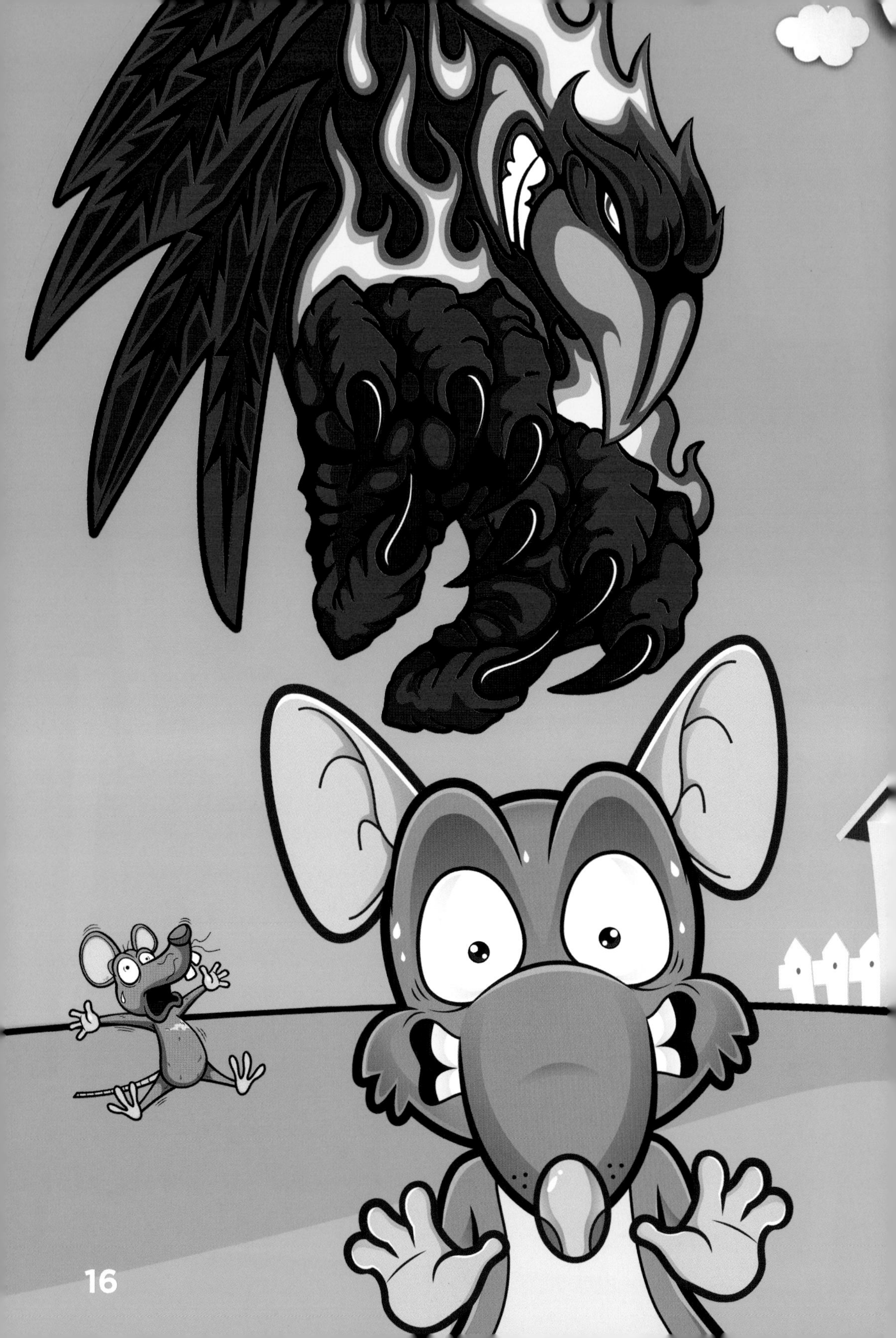

Phoenix Food

Feeding a phoenix is probably the easiest part of owning one. Simply let your phoenix hunt **rodents** near your house. The bird will go after mice, rats, and moles. It might even bring you some as presents. These gifts might be gross, but make sure you appreciate them. You'll hurt your phoenix's feelings if you don't!

Chunks of fish make special treats. The smellier, the better!

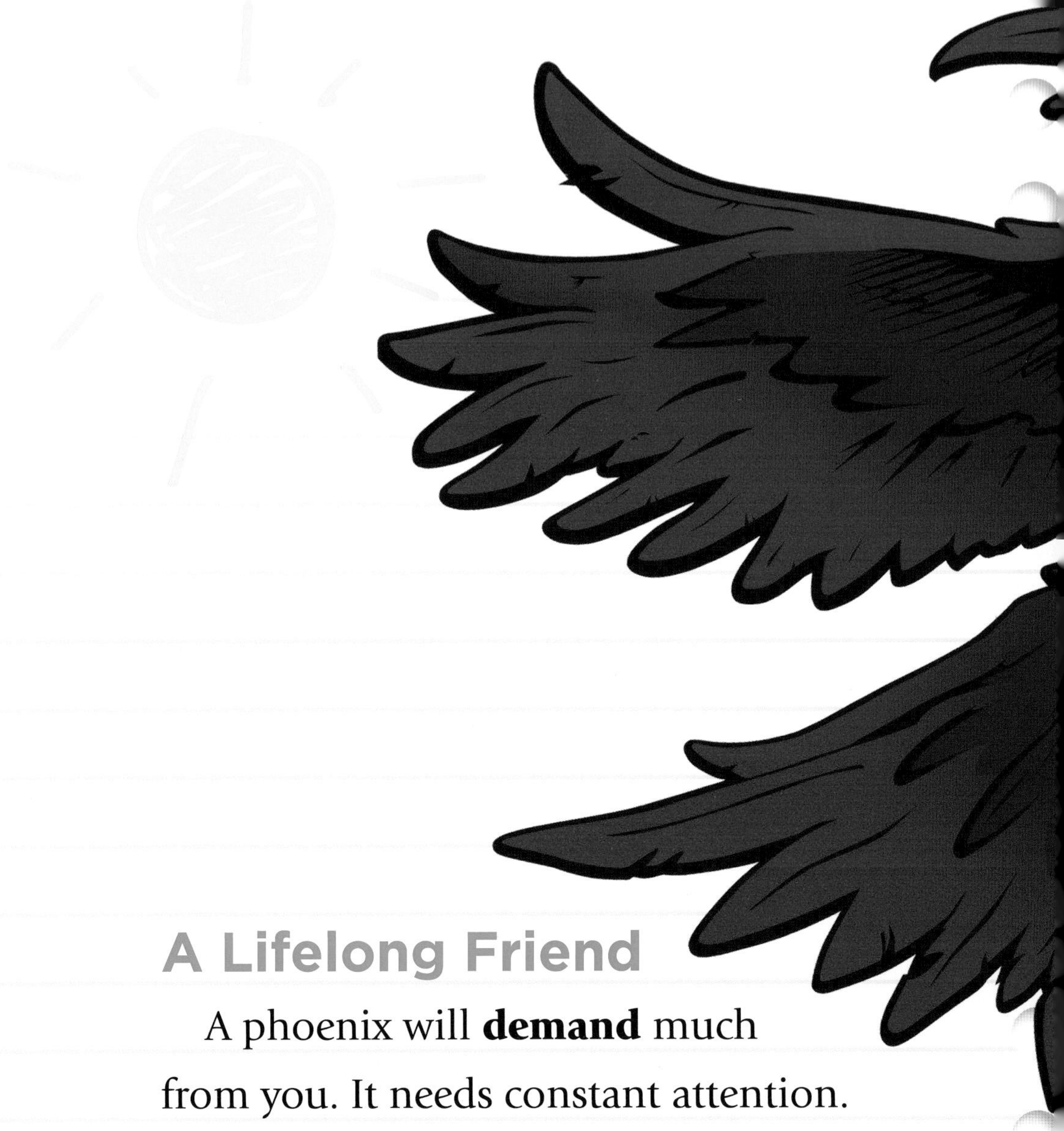

A Lifelong Friend

A phoenix will **demand** much from you. It needs constant attention. Its space needs regular cleaning. But your phoenix will also fill your life with beauty. It'll be a good friend. If you can handle the challenges, a phoenix might be right for you.

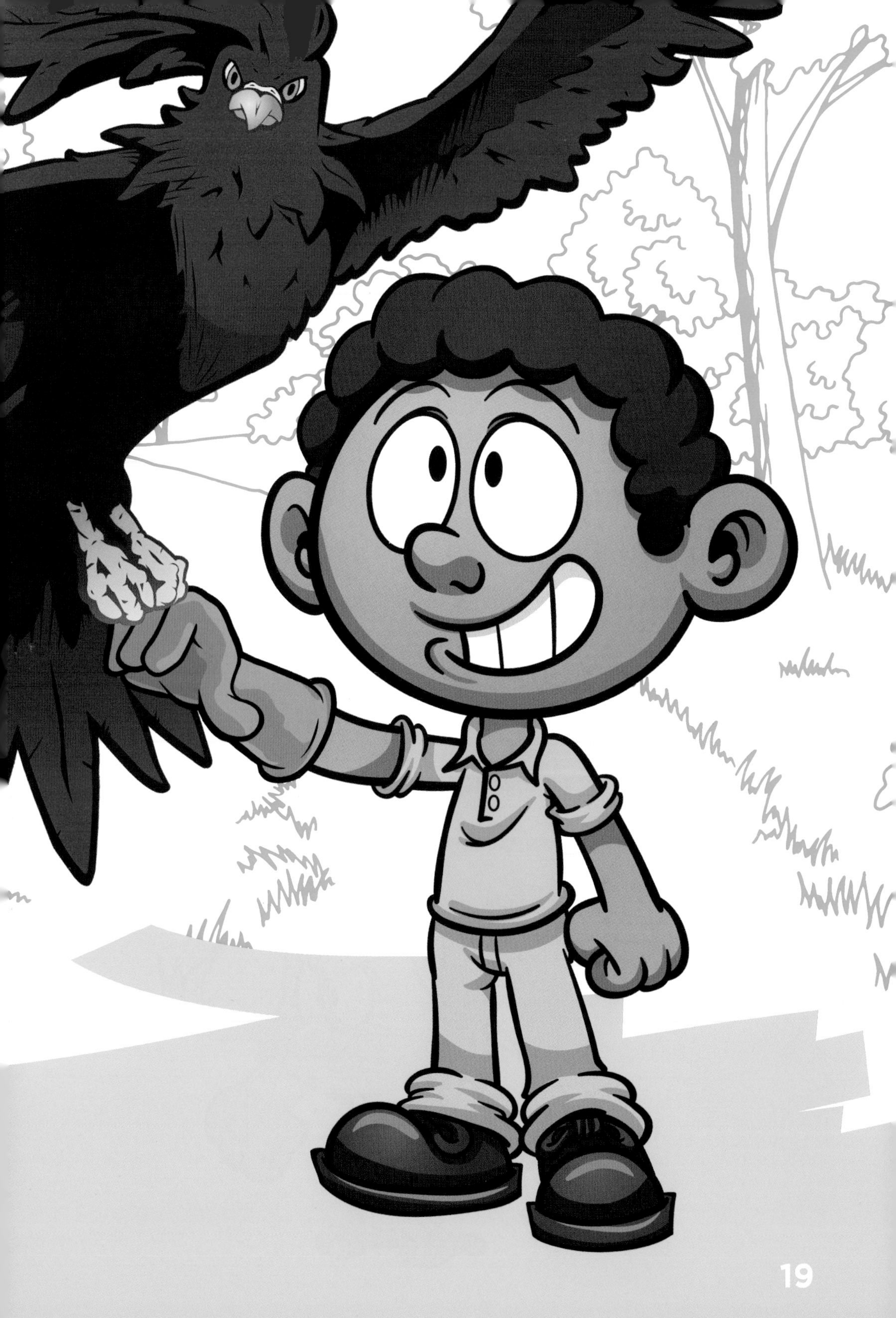

Chapter 4
Get in on the
Hi Jinx

No birds really burn up and come back to life. But people have seen birds using fire in a smart way. Some birds in Australia pick up burning branches. The birds bring the fire to areas where **prey** live. Animals run from the flames. When they do, the birds grab them. People call these birds firehawks. Imagine having a pet like that!

Take It One Step More

1. Many people enjoy stories about phoenixes and other magical creatures. Why do you think that is?

2. Would you like a pet that needs so much attention? Why or why not?

3. What would be the hardest part about owning a phoenix?

GLOSSARY

admire (ad-MAHYUHR)—to think very highly of

demand (dee-MAND)—to say or ask something in a very forceful way

mystical (MIS-ti-kuhl)—having a spiritual meaning that is difficult to see or understand

pamper (PAM-per)—to treat someone or something with great care and attention

prey (PRAY)—an animal hunted or killed for food

radiate (REY-dee-eyt)—to send out rays

rodent (RO-dent)—a small gnawing mammal, such as a mouse, squirrel, or beaver

LEARN MORE

BOOKS

Lawrence, Sandra, and Stuart Hill. *The Atlas of Monsters: Mythical Creatures from around the World.* Philadelphia: Running Press Kids, 2019.

Marsico, Katie. *Beastly Monsters: From Dragons to Griffins.* Monster Mania. Minneapolis: Lerner Publications, 2017.

Sautter, A.J. *Discover Harpies, Minotaurs, and Other Mythical Fantasy Beasts.* All about Fantasy Creatures. North Mankato, MN: Capstone Press, 2018.

WEBSITES

Phoenix
www.britannica.com/topic/phoenix-mythological-bird

Phoenix Bird Facts and History
mocomi.com/what-is-phoenix/

Phoenix (Mythology) Facts for Kids
kids.kiddle.co/Phoenix_(mythology)

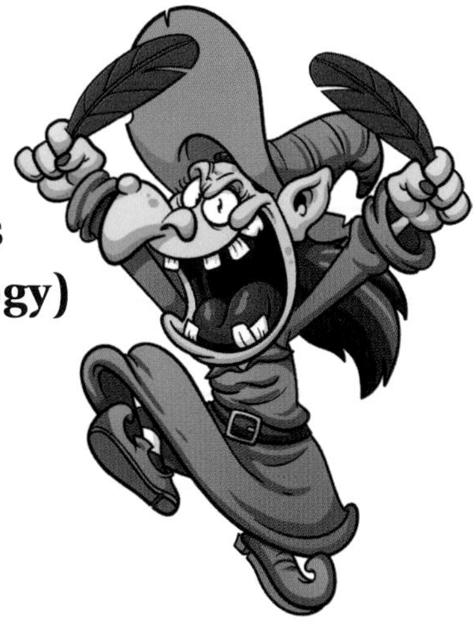

INDEX